Technical assistance and pie expertise provided by Jane Albin.

THIS IS A BORZOI BOOK PUBLISHED BY ALFRED A. KNOPF

Visit us on the Web! www.randomhouse.com/kids

Educators and librarians, for a variety of teaching tools, visit us at www.randomhouse.com/teachers

Library of Congress Cataloging-in-Publication Data
Priceman, Marjorie.
How to make a cherry pie and see the U.S.A. / Marjorie Priceman — 1st ed.
    p. cm.
Summary: Since the Cook Shop is closed, the reader is led around the United States to gather coal, cotton, granite, and other natural resources needed to make the utensils for preparing a cherry pie.
ISBN 978-0-375-81255-2 (trade) — ISBN 978-0-375-91255-9 (lib. bdg.)
[1. Natural resources—Fiction. 2. U.S. states—Fiction. 3. Voyages and travels—Fiction. 4. Baking—Fiction. 5. Humorous stories.]
I. Title. II. Title: How to make a cherry pie and see the USA.
PZ7.P932Hk 2008
[E]—dc22
2007046064

The text of this book is set in 16-point Goudy.
The illustrations in this book were created using gouache on hot-pressed watercolor paper.

MANUFACTURED IN MALAYSIA
October 2008
10 9 8 7 6 5 4 3 2 1

First Edition

How to Make a Cherry Pie and see the U.S.A.

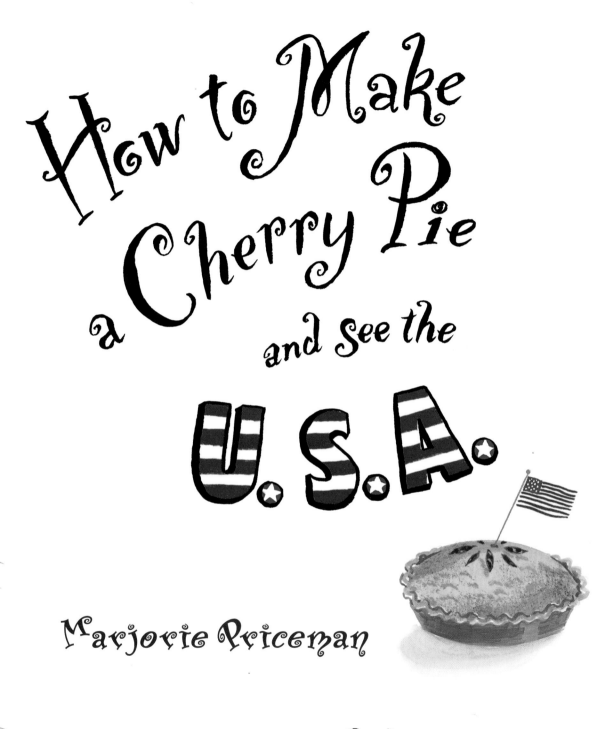

Marjorie Priceman

ALFRED A. KNOPF New York

Cherry Pie

(ask an adult to help)

CRUST

2 cups all-purpose flour

1 teaspoon salt

2/3 cup chilled vegetable shortening

2 tablespoons chilled butter

4 tablespoons ice water

Preheat the oven to 425 degrees Fahrenheit (218 degrees Celsius).

Combine the flour and salt in a large bowl. Combine the shortening and butter in a small bowl. Spoon half of the shortening mixture into the flour mixture, then use the tips of your fingers to lightly work it in until the dough has the texture of cornmeal. Add the remaining shortening and work it in until the dough forms pea-sized pieces. Sprinkle ice water lightly on the dough. Gently lift and turn the ingredients with a spoon or your hands to spread the water. If you can form the dough into a neat ball, stop handling it. (If it falls apart, add a little more water.) Lightly flour your rolling pin and pastry slab or counter. Form the dough into two equal balls. Press one into a patty on your pastry slab. Roll in one direction (not to and fro) from the center out to the edge. When the dough is 1/8 inch thick, transfer it to the pie pan. Gently press the crust into place. Roll out the second ball of dough in the same way (this is the top crust). Cut some steam vents using the side of a spoon.

FILLING

1 cup sugar

2 tablespoons flour

1/8 teaspoon salt

4 cups (1 quart) fresh or canned
    sour cherries, pitted

In a large bowl, mix the sugar, flour, and salt. Add the cherries (if using canned cherries, drain the liquid first). Toss to cover the cherries with the sugar mixture. Gently spoon the filling into the bottom crust.

Place the top crust on the pie. (If the crust tears, just arrange the pieces on top.) Fold over any excess dough at the edges, then crimp with your finger or a spoon handle. Place the pie on the lowest oven rack. Bake for 10 minutes, then reduce the heat to 350 degrees Fahrenheit (177 degrees Celsius). Continue baking for 30 to 40 minutes, or until the crust is lightly browned. With your pot holders, remove the pie and allow to cool before serving.

In the mood for a cherry pie? Let's get started. First, mix flour and salt in a bowl. What, no bowl? You will definitely need a bowl. Also, a pie pan, a rolling pin, a measuring cup, a pastry slab, a set of spoons, and some pot holders—which you can get at the Cook Shop.

But if the Cook Shop happens
to be closed . . .

WEST

Go to New York and hail a taxi. Ask the driver to drop you off at the corner of Pennsylvania and Ohio.

Then find the closest coal mine. Coal is used to make steel, and you need steel to make your pie pan. Take the trolley deep underground and fill a bucket to the brim. Don't forget your hard hat and flashlight!

Next, ride a riverboat down the Mississippi.
(It takes as long to sail it as to spell it.)

RIVER QUEEN

If the boat docks in Louisiana at lunchtime, eat
a bowl of gumbo. Then go to a cotton farm and
pick an armful of cotton for your pot holders.

Catch an express bus to New Mexico. If the bus stops at the northwest corner of the state, take the opportunity to be four places at once.

UTAH

COLORADO

ARIZONA

NEW MEXICO

That was fun. Now back to work. Your task
is to find some clay. A good place to look is
down—you're probably standing on it! Dig up
enough clay to make a mixing bowl. (Look out
for cactus needles!)

Board a train to Washington, the only state
named for a president, the only president
rumored to have a set of wooden teeth!
Speaking of wood, go to the forest and find
a nice branch. Saw off a piece the size of a
rolling pin and then . . .

ATTENTION!
WE INTERRUPT THIS BOOK TO
REPORT THAT YOU HAVE WON
AN ALL-EXPENSES-PAID TRIP
TO HAWAII! YOUR SHIP
WILL LEAVE TODAY
FROM CALIFORNIA.
HURRY!! ALOHA!!!

CALIFORNIA

(This is great news because you need sand, and
Hawaii has plenty of it. Glass is made from sand,
and you need glass to make your measuring cup.)
Fill a pail with sand. Watch out for falling coconuts!

Make your way to New Hampshire for granite. New Hampshire can usually be found between Maine and Vermont. Granite can usually be found on the sides of steep mountains. Rappel down the side of a mountain and chisel a chunk of granite for your pastry slab.

Next stop, Texas. To get to Texas, follow the coastline south. When you hit Florida, turn right. Then go straight until you run into a longhorn steer. Ask the steer directions to an oil field.

Plastic is made from oil, and you'll need about a quart to make your spoons. Tip your hat to the oil workers, then head to the airport.

TEXAS

FLORIDA

Board a plane flying north. When you're over South Dakota, don't forget to wave to the presidents.

Then chill out in Alaska—*just because it's there.*
After you've seen the scenery, hurry home.

Now all you have to do is:

Process the coal, mix with iron, and roll into flat sheets. Form the sheets into a pie pan.

Spin the cotton into thread. Weave the thread into cloth. Cut and stitch the cloth into pot holders.

Carve the wood into a rolling pin, then sand and seal.

Shape the clay into a bowl. Paint with glaze, then fire.

Process the oil and pour into spoon-shaped molds.

Cut the granite into a square pastry slab, then smooth and polish.

Melt the sand until it liquefies, then pour into a measuring-cup mold.

Next, using your bowl, spoons, rolling pin, measuring cup, pie pan, pastry slab, and pot holders, mix the ingredients and bake the pie.

When the pie has cooled, cut into slices with a pie server. If you don't have a pie server, you can get one at the Cook Shop.

But if the Cook Shop is *still* closed . . .